Licensed exclusively to Top That Publishing Ltd
Tide Mill Way, Woodbridge, Suffolk, IP12 1AP, UK
www.topthatpublishing.com
Copyright © 2013 Tide Mill Media
All rights reserved
2 4 6 8 9 7 5 3 1
Manufactured in China

Written by Oakley Graham
Illustrated by Sanja Rescek

ISBN 978-1-78244-354-4

A catalogue record for this book is available from the British Library

The Little Rock Light

Written by Oakley Graham

Illustrated by Sanja Rescek

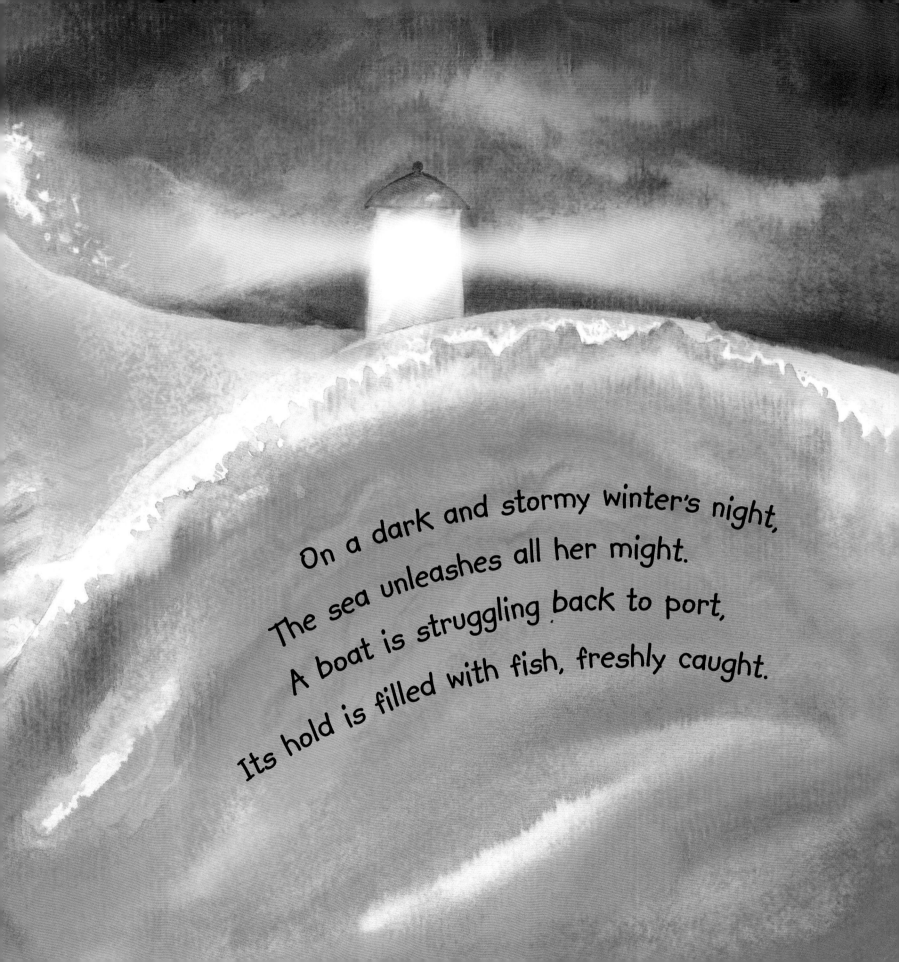

On a dark and stormy winter's night,
The sea unleashes all her might.
A boat is struggling back to port,
Its hold is filled with fish, freshly caught.

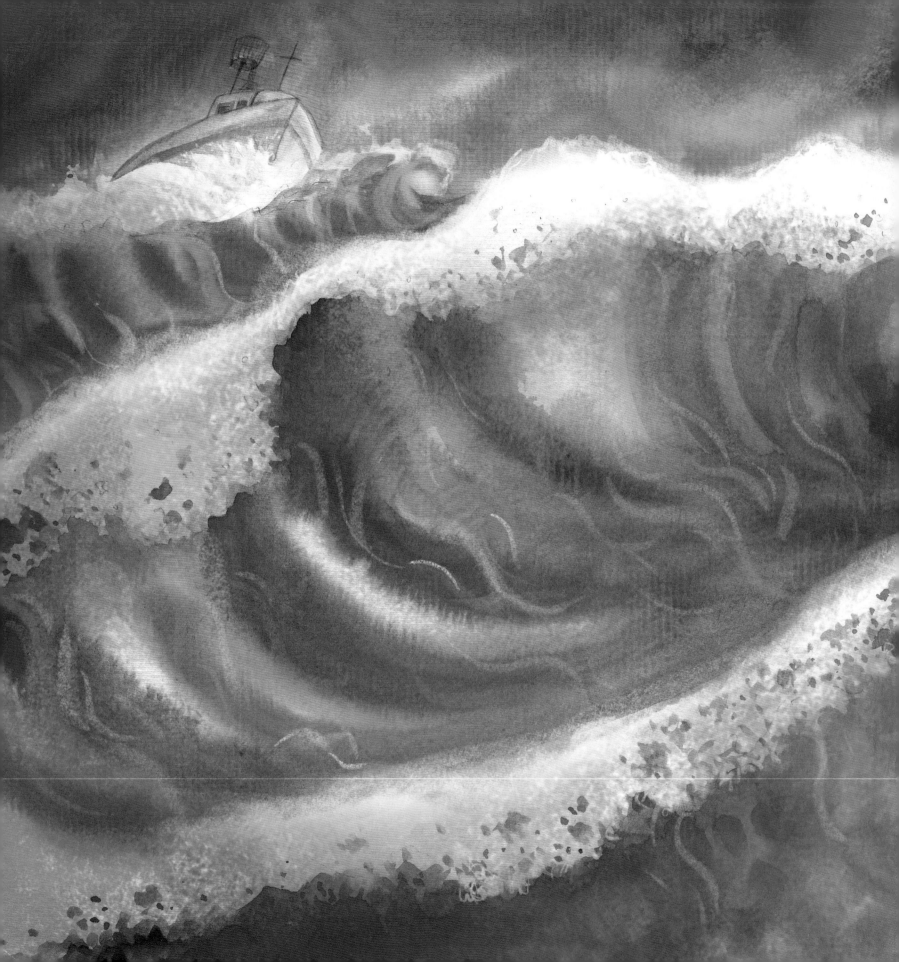

The waves rear up, crash and thunder,
The boat stays afloat, and avoids going under.
The captain searches for a guiding light,
To help him in his desperate plight.

The rain lashes down, the wind is howling,
A pod of hungry whales are prowling.

The boat is tossed from side to side,
As it battles against the unruly tide.

The captain avoids a dreadful shock,
When he spies seals resting on jagged rocks.
Then a light cuts through the inky black,
To help the boat get back on track.

Like a sequence from an amazing dream,
Dolphins glide through the moonlight beam.

The crew look to the steadfast light above,
And think of the people they dearly love.

The night recedes, the sun will soon be rising,
But still the powerful light keeps shining.

The waves are now just a distant roar,
As otters play happily by the shore.

A flock of gulls screech overhead,
The early morning sky is a vivid red.

The light guides them safely home,
Through the flotsam and the foam.

The boat is safely back in the port,
And the captain reflects on a comforting thought.

Whether you are a friend, or a visiting stranger,
The Little Rock Light will keep you from danger.